African Methodist Episcopal Church

Minutes of the Seventeenth Session

of the Florida Annual Conference of the African Methodist Episcopal

Church

African Methodist Episcopal Church

Minutes of the Seventeenth Session
of the Florida Annual Conference of the African Methodist Episcopal Church

ISBN/EAN: 9783337361686

Printed in Europe, USA, Canada, Australia, Japan

Cover: Foto ©Andreas Hilbeck / pixelio.de

More available books at **www.hansebooks.com**

MINUTES

OF THE

SEVENTEENTH SESSION

OF

The Florida Annual Conference

OF THE

African Methodist Episcopal Church,

HELD IN THE

A. M. E. CHURCH, AT MONTICELLO, FLORIDA,

From Nov. 29th to Dec. 6th. 1882.

PRICE, - - - - - - 10c. PER COPY.

A. W. WAYMAN, D. D., Presiding Bishop,
No. 127 East Baltimore St., Baltimore, Md.

A. J. KERSHAW, Secretary, - - - Greenwood, Fla.

**A. B. DUDLEY, Chairman Publishing Com., Marianna, Fla.

PUBLISHED BY

LATIMER C. VAUGHAN,

Editor and Proprietor of

The Marianna Courier.

THE MARIANNA COURIER is the only paper published in the five Eastern Counties of West Florida, and as an advertising medium, it has few superiors: at its office all kinds of Printing is done. Printing of Minutes a specialty. Address the Publisher for further information.

CONFERENCE PROCEEDINGS.

. FIRST DAY.

MONTICELLO, FLORIDA, *November* 29, 1882.

The 17th session of the FLORIDA ANNUAL CONFERENCE of the A. M. E. Church, convened in the A. M. E. Church at Monticello, on the above named date, at 10 o'clock A. M.

After singing and prayer, the Bishop read the 13th chapter of 1st Corinthians, and made some interesting and instructive remarks thereon, to which the Conference listened with marked attention.

After this, S. L. Mims, Secretary of the last Conference, called the roll, and the members answered to their names.

The election of secretaries being in order, on motion of S. L. Mims, A. J. KERSHAW was elected Secretary; and on motion of G. W. Witherspoon, D. QUARTERMAN was elected Statistical Secretary. THOS. MOORER was elected Recording Secretary.

The Bishop announced the following committees:

On Finance—J. H. Spears, T. Moorer, F. White, J. Taylor.

On Temperance—A. B. Dudley, L. Hargret, Geo. Anderson.

To Receive Dollar Money—G. W. Witherspoon, F. White, J. P. Campbell, S. L. C. Dawson.

On Education—M. A. Trapp, J. H. Gilbert, M. M. Moore, V. B. Brooks.

Sabbath Schools—B. C. Gibbs, I. Buggs, C. B. Green, F. J. Thompson.

Post-Office—J. H. Holland.

To Receive Mite Missionary—R. Meacham.

To Receive Missionary Money—E. W. Johnson, P. Crooms, C. L. Lane, J. Taylor.

Superannuated Preachers, Widows and Orphans—F. Lavette, S. W. Frazer, W. A. Burch, George Anderson.

Circuits, Stations and Missions—The Presiding Elders.

On Publication Department—E. R. Robertson, M. M. Moore, F. J. Thompson, A. Attaway.

P. Crooms moved to have a committee appointed to receive Minute money; and after much discussion in regard to said motion, both *pro* and *con.*, the motion was lost when put upon its passage.

On motion of S. L. Mims, the Conference agreed to have one session per day—from 9 A. M. to 2 P. M.

On motion of R. Meacham, the bar of Conference was fixed at fifth pew from the altar.

W. H. Powell, J. A. Cary and J. H. King, all of Georgia Conference, were introduced to the Conference by the Bishop and invited within the bar of Conference.

The account of the manager of Publication Department was presented to the Conference; and on motion of A. J. Kershaw, was delivered to A. B. Dudley for collection. The said account was the several brethren's indebtedness to the Publication Department.

L. W. Allen and S. W. Frazer were elected Marshals; also E. W. Johnson and W. C. Hamilton were appointed ushers.

The Bishop instructed the Presiding Elders to report their several candidates for admission to the proper committee.

S. L. Mims moved that a special collection be taken up on Thursday, November 30th, at 11 o'clock A. M., for the benefit of the Metropolitan Church at Washington, D. C., and be immediately forwarded to J. H. Handy, pastor of said church; which motion prevailed.

The committees on the several years' studies instructed the respective Classes to meet them at 4 o'clock P. M., at the church, for the purpose of passing their examination.

The Committee on Public Worship reported that R. Meacham would preach the Annual Sermon at 7½ o'clock; and F. Lavette would preach at the Missionary Baptist Church at the same hour.

The hour of 2 P. M. having arrived, the benediction was pronounced by W. H. Powell, and Conference adjourned to meet at 7½ P. M. to hear the annual sermon.

At half-past 7, Elder R. Meacham preached the annual sermon from the text: "Go ye and teach all nations." A sermon that was well delivered, and well received by an attentive audience.

On motion, the Conference adjourned to meet the following morning at 9 o'clock.

SECOND DAY.

MONTICELLO, FLORIDA, *November* 30, 1882.

The Conference met pursuant to adjournment. Bishop Wayman called the body to order. The roll was called, and the brethren answered to their names.

The journal of the first day's session was read, corrected and approved.

The Bishop called upon each Presiding Elder to state the ministerial standing of their respective Districts.

S. L. Mims reported Monticello District as standing fair, with four exceptions; and these four cases were referred to two committees, consisting of Thomas Moorer, J. H. Gilbert and D. Quarterman, constituting No. 1; John Speight, Joseph H. Spears and S. L. C. Dawson, constituting No. 2.

R. Meacham reported Tallahassee District **in good order,** and its ministers standing fair.

H. Call reported Marianna District in good condition, and ministers standing fair, with one exception

W. **L.** G. Jones reported his (the Pensacola) District as not in a very good condition, owing to the visitation of the yellow fever during the past year; but the ministers all standing fair.

A communication from Theo. Gould, of the Publication Department, A. M. E. Church, was received, read and given to the Committee on Publication Department; also a letter from B. W. Roberts, of Pensacola, Fla., which was read by the Secretary, and ordered noted upon the minutes of the Conference.

The hour of 11 o'clock having arrived, the Conference took a recess to hear the Thanksgiving Sermon; which was preached by Bishop A. W. Wayman, from the 145th Psalm, 8th and 9th verses, and was much appreciated by the Conference and congregation.

After which a collection was taken up, amounting to $11.10, for the benefit of the Metropolitan A. M. E. Church at Washington, D. C.; which was turned over to W. A. Bird to hold until further orders.

C. H. Pearce, from the East Florida Conference, was introduced to the Conference and invited within the bar.

The Committee on Public Worship reported that W. H. Powell would preach at half-past 7 P. M.

Conference adjourned. Benediction by Charles H. Pearce.

THIRD DAY.

MONTICELLO, FLORIDA, *December* 1, 1882.

Conference met pursuant to adjournment. Religious exercises conducted by Bro. I. Buggs.

The Chairman ordered the roll called, and the members answered to their names.

On motion of A. B. Dudley, the journal of the previous day was read, corrected and approved.

After which the Bishop called up the

DISCIPLINARY QUESTIONS.

Question 6th—What preachers are admitted on trial? Harris Humphreys, John Dash, Henry Starks, A. B. Collins, K. P. Neal, Fagan Petters, Charles Spires.

Question 7th—Who remain on trial? S. W. Frazer, P. Johnson, James Clark, W. Washington, J. E. Roberts, Serry Lewis, Noah Randolph, R. Raymon, L. W. Allen, G. W. Wynne, F. J. Thompson, S. C. Clary, W. A. Burch.

Question 8th—Who are admitted or re-admitted into full connection? B. C. Gibbs, J. P. Campbell, E. R. Robinson, W. C. Hamilton, C. L. Lane, S. C. Clary.

Question 9th—Who are the Deacons? (See Roll.)

Question 10th—Who have been elected and ordained Deacons and Elders this year? Elders: E. W. Johnson and I. Buggs. Local Deacons: F. Jones and C. L. Lane.

Question 11th—Who have located this year? None.

Question 12th—Who have been elected by the General Conference to exercise the Episcopal office and superintend the A. M. E. Church? D. A. Payne, A. W. Wayman, J. P. Campbell, J. A. Shorter, T. M. D. Ward, J. M. Brown, H. M. Turner, W. F. Dickenson, R. H. Cain.

Question 13th—Who are the supernumerary and superannuated? J. Churchill, supernumerary.

Question 14th—Who have been expelled from the connection this year? None.

Question 15th—Who have withdrawn from the connection this year? None.

Question 16th—Are all the preachers blameless in life and conversation? All seem to stand fair.

Question 17th—Who have died this year? None.

Question 18th—Where are the preachers stationed this year? (See Appointments.)

Question 19th—Where shall our next Conference be held? Upon the asking of this question, R. Meacham nominated Tallahassee. J. Speight nominated Appalachicola. G. W. Witherspoon nominated Pensacola.

After the vote was taken, the Chairman declared Pensacola to be the seat of our next Annual Conference.

A letter was received from Mr. Landrum, of Pensacola, relative to our last Annual Conference Minutes, which was read.

On motion of S. L. Mims, each minister was requested to pay one dollar for the printing of said minutes; which motion prevailed, and said collection was postponed until Saturday morning.

The Bishop requested the Presiding Elders to present the recommendations of the applicants for admission.

The Committee on Public Worship reported that D. Quarterman would preach at A. M. E. Church at 7½ o'clock P. M.

This being done, Conference adjourned to meet Saturday morning, 9 o'clock. Benediction by W. L. G. Jones.

FOURTH DAY.

MONTICELLO, FLORIDA, *December* 2, 1882.

Conference convened at 9 o'clock A. M. Bishop Wayman in the chair. Religious exercises conducted by W. L. G. Jones.

Roll called, and members answered to their names. Journal of previous day read, corrected and approved.

On motion of G. W. Witherspoon, the Electoral College of the Florida Annual Conference was called to meet at Tallahassee, Fla., the second Wednesday in July, 1883.

The Committee on charges and complaints reported that they having examined into the case of M. A. Trapp, it was referred back to the Conference for its consideration.

The Committee on Education made their report, which was received and adopted.

The Committee on Temperance made their report, which was received and adopted.

The Committee on the Publication Department made their report, which was received and adopted.

The Committee on Superannuated Preachers, Widows and Orphans, made their report; said report was postponed until Monday morning for further action.

On motion, Forney Jones was elected to Local Deacon's orders.

The recommendation of Bro. W. J. Watson was received, and he admitted on trial.

On motion of S. L. Mims, the name of Bro. R. H. Munroe was dropped from the roll.

In the case of G. W. Witherspoon *vs.* M. M. Moore, the Conference ordered M. M. Moore to return G. W. Witherspoon's panorama to him forthwith.

Elder Pasco, of the M. E. Church, South, was introduced to the Conference, and invited within the bar of Conference.

The Committee on Public Worship reported that Brother Collier would preach at A. M. E. Church at 7½ o'clock P. M.

Also for Sabbath they made the following report:

A. M. E. Church, 11 A. M., Bishop Wayman. At 3 P. M., H. Call. At 7½ P. M., C. H. Pearce.

Bailey's Hall, 3 P. M., Bishop Wayman. At 11 A. M., J. H. **Spears.** At 7½ P. M., J. H. Gilbert.

M. E. Church, 3 P. M., J. Speight. At 7½ P. M., A. B. Dudley.

Missionary Baptist Church, 11 A. M., C. Brown. At **3 P. M.,** F. Lavette. At 7½ P. M., T. Moorer.

The hour of 2 P. M. came, and Conference took a recess until 4 o'clock; at which hour Conference convened to hear the case of Annie Davis vs. A. R. Hansberry. After hearing the testimony, the Conference found Brother Hansberry guilty, and he was accordingly expelled from the connection. The defendant gave notice that he would take an appeal.

Conference adjourned to meet at 9 o'clock Monday morning.

FIFTH DAY.

MONTICELLO, FLORIDA, *December* 4, 1882.

Conference met pursuant to adjournment. Bishop Wayman in the chair. Religious exercises conducted by J. Taylor.

The calling of the roll was omitted. The journal of the previous day was read, corrected and approved.

On motion of S. L. Mims, the Finance Committee was ordered to pay $3.60 for freight on a package of books known as the "Budget."

S. L. Mims moved to reconsider the action by which A. R. Hansberry was expelled; which motion was carried, and after a re-hearing of the case, Brother Hansberry was found not guilty, and was restored to good standing in the Conference.

Conference adjourned until 3 o'clock.

When the above hour arrived, Conference resumed its session to witness the Sunday School celebration; which was addressed by F. White and J. Taylor.

After this Conference took up the case of Mrs. Hannah Scipline vs. M. A. Trapp, and after a three hours trial the said M. A. Trapp was found not guilty, and his character passed.

The Conference Missionary Society met, and after collecting the annual fees from its members, proceeded to elect officers for the year 1883:

President—A. W. Wayman, D. D.

Vice President—Fuller White.

Secretary—Thomas Moorer.

Treasurer—C. Brown.

Board of Directors—R. Meacham, W. A. Bird, D. Quarterman, H. Call.

Isaac Buggs, the Conference Book Steward, made his report, which was received and adopted.

The Bishop gave notice that the "Conference Literary Society" would meet at 3 o'clock P. M., Tuesday.

Elder A. B. Dudley was elected Conference Book Steward for 1883.

The Bishop notified the Board of Directors of the Conference Missionary Society to meet him at the parsonage at 7 o'clock Tuesday morning, for the purpose of making disbursement of the Missionary money.

On motion of A. J. Kershaw, $18.16, which is forty per cent. of the Missionary money, be forwarded to J. M. Townsend, per Bishop Wayman.

Conference adjourned to meet Tuesday, 8 o'clock A. M.

SIXTH DAY.

MONTICELLO, FLORIDA, December 5, 1882.

Conference met pursuant to adjournment. Bishop A. W. Wayman, presiding. Religious services conducted by Bro. G. W. T. Wynns.

Minutes of previous day read, corrected and approved.

The Conference raised $30.31 for printing the Minutes of 1883; the said sum was turned over to Elder A. B. Dudley, chairman and treasurer of the Committee on Publication.

On motion of A. J. Kershaw, the $6.85 of Educational money was added to the $11.10 of the "Metropolitan" money, and sent to Rev. J. A. Handy, of Washington, D. C., for the benefit of the Metropolitan A. M. E. Church, of said city.

The hour of 11 o'clock came. Elder C. H. Pearce preached the Ordination Sermon. After which the following persons were ordained Deacons and Elders:

DEACONS—S. W. Frazier, G. W. T. Wynns and C. L. Lane.
LOCAL DEACONS—Forney Jones and Berry Cromidy.
ELDERS—Isaac Buggs and E. W. Johnson.

On motion of G. W. Witherspoon, A. J. Kershaw, D. Quarterman, Thomas Moorer and A. B. Dudley were appointed a committee to publish the Minutes of the Conference.

After which the Conference adjourned to meet in Pensacola.

Appointments for 1883.

MONTICELLO DISTRICT—A. Attaway, P. E.

Monticello Station, H. Call.
Ancilla Circuit, A. R. Hansberry.
Waukeenah Circuit, Geo. Anderson.
Thompson Valley " Geo. Washington.
Turkey Scratch, E. W. Johnson.
Monticello Mission, H. B. DeVaughn.
Centenary Circuit, W. C. Hamilton.
Station One " Wm. Washington.
Gum Swamp " Isaac Buggs.
Concord, Leon Co., J. H. Spears.
Mount Olive Circuit, W. A. Bird.

TALLAHASSEE DISTRICT—F. White, P. E.

Tallahassee Station, A. A. Price.
Tallahassee Mission, L. W. Allen.
St. John Circuit, S. W. Frazier.
Quincy Station, D. Quarterman.
Concord Circuit, J. P. Campbell.
Rock Comfort, N. Randolph.
Midway Circuit, G. W. Wynn.
Imonia Slough, M. J. Watson.
Chattahoochee, Peter Crooms.
Walker Mission, Henry Starks, Jr.
Lake Jackson, E. R. Roberson.
Wakulla Mission, H. Humphries.
Centreville, C. Brown.

MARIANNA DISTRICT—Thomas Moorer, P. E.

Marianna Station, R. Meacham.
Antioch Circuit, L. Hargret.
Pope Chapel Mission, John Dash.
Campbellton Station, F. Lavette.
Springfield Circuit, M. A. Trapp.
Greenwood Circuit, A. J. Kershaw.
Mt. Olive and Jerusalem, E. Smith.
Liberty County Circuit, K. P. Neal.
Bethlehem Circuit, A. B. Dudley.
Apalachicola Station, John Speight.
St. Rose Mission, A. Godwin.
Calhoun Mission, C. L. Clory.
Carribella and Rico, A. Hammonds.

PENSACOLA DISTRICT—W. L. G. JONES, P. E.

Pensacola Station, G. W. Witherspoon. *St. Luke Circuit*, S. L. C. Dawson.
Molina and Oakfield, F. J. Thompson. *Silvana and Orange*, J. H. Holland.
Walton County Circuit, W. A. Burch. *St. Marys and Milltown*, R. Raymon.
Millview Circuit, C. L. Lane. *Milton Station*, B. C. Gibbs.
Navy Yard Circuit, C. B. Green *Magnolia Mission*, John Taylor.

CONFERENCE ROOM, MONTICELLO, FLA., Dec. 4, 1882.

This is to certify that Rev. M. M. Moore, an Elder in good and regular standing in the Florida Annual Conference of the African M. E. Church, is transferred to the Georgia Conference of the same.

A. W. WAYMAN, Presiding Bishop.

CONFERENCE ROOM, MONTICELLO, FLA., Dec. 4, 1882.

This is to certify that Rev. S. L. Mims, J. H. Gilbert and B. W. Roberts, all Elders in good and regular standing in the Florida Annual Conference of the A. M. E. Church, are transferred to the Alabama Conference of the same.

A. W. WAYMAN, Presiding **Bishop.**

MONTICELLO, FLA., December 5, 1882.

This is to certify that the following persons were ordained Deacons, viz.: G. W. T. Wynns, Forney Jones, C. L. Lane, B. Cromidy and S. W. Frazier; and also the following were ordained Elders by me: Isaac Buggs and Edward W. Johnson.

A. W. WAYMAN, Presiding Bishop.

Whereas, we, the members of the Florida Conference, have learned that it is the intention of the presiding Bishop to transfer from this Conference our beloved colleagues, Rev. S. L. Mims, John H. Gilbert and Morris M. Moore; therefore

Resolved, That after several years of pleasant association, we reluctantly part with them, and in so doing we commend them to God and the word of his grace.

Resolved, further, That those brethren leaving with them, have our best wishes for their future welfare; and should they ever return, we shall gladly receive them. A. J. KERSHAW.

Whereas, Bishop Wayman has, with profound dignity, presided over our deliberations to the satisfaction of all the brethren; and whereas, the good people of this community have spared no pains to make every thing pleasant for all; therefore, be it

Resolved, That we tender to this entire community our heart-felt thanks, and hereafter promise, wherever we go, to remember them at a throne of grace. G. W. WITHERSPOON.

Resolved, That each minister bring to the next Annual Conference the sum of one dollar for the printing of the minutes. Any minister failing to bring said dollar, the same shall be taken out of his missionary money. D. QUARTERMAN.

PENSACOLA, FLA., November 27, 1882.

To the Bishop and Conference:—Rev. Father and Brethren:—It is with regret that I must inform you that I can not meet you all this Conference on account of the epidemic that visited our city, which left destitution, poverty and death in its wake. Yet we can say, thanks be to God, who saith to his people, we are left here to suffer a little while longer ; but we hope it will not be long before we will come up again. We would fraternally ask the Conference to help us, if it is only ten dollars, to assist us in completing our church. We have a piece of property that we can justly say that we are proud of. We have it all completed excepting the seats, which will be ordered made as soon as possible.

We are all anxious to have the Bishop visit us as soon as possible.
Yours, in the bonds of the Gospel,   B. W. ROBERTS,
Pastor **A. M.** E. Church.

TO BE ADMITTED ON TRIAL.

FIRST YEAR.

Harrison Humphries,	John Dash,	Henry Starks, Jr.
Fagan Peters,	A. B. Collins,	K. P. Neal,
Charles Spires,	M. J. Watson.	

TO BE ADMITTED TO FULL CONNECTION.

SECOND YEAR'S CLASS.

C. B. Green.	B. C. Gibbs,	J. P. Campbell,
E. R. Robinson,	Paris Johnson,	W. C. Hamilton,
C. L. Lane,	S. C. Clary.	

COMMITTEES OF EXAMINATION.

To Examine the First Class—C. Brown, Wm. A. Bird, E. W. Johnson.

To Examine Second Year's Class—H. Call, A. B. Dudley, Isaac Buggs.

To Examine Third Year's Class—R. Meacham, M. A. Trapp, A. R. Hansberry.

To Examine Fourth Year's Class—D. Quarterman, J. Speight, F. Lavette.

To Examine Candidates for Admission—G. W. Witherspoon, L. Hargett, P. Croom.

To Examine Local Preachers for Deacons' Orders—Joseph H. Spears, E. Smith, George Anderson.

To Preach the Annual Sermon—A. Attaway.

To Preach the Missionary Sermon—Thomas Moorer.

COMMITTEES WHO EXAMINED LAST YEAR.

To Examine Candidates for Admission—A. R. Hansberry, Edmund Smith, Peter Crooms.

To Examine Candidates in First Year's Class—M. A. Trapp, A. B. Dudley, John Speight. Candidates as follows—S. W. Frazier, William Washington, J. E. Roberts, Surry Lewis, Noah Randolph, Robert Raymon, Lewis W. Allen, G. W. T. Wynn, F. J. Thompson, W. A. Burch, James Clark.

To Examine Candidates in Second Year's Class—Joseph H. Spears, A. J. Kershaw, J. H. Gilbert. Candidates as follows—C. B. Green, B. C. Gibbs, S. C. A. Clary, J. P. Campbell, E. W. Roberson, J. H. Holland, R. H. Monroe, J. Quarterman, P. Johnson, W. C. Hamilton, T. W. Dockins, C. Lane.

To Examine Candidates in Third Year's Studies—Thomas Moorer, W. A. Bird, F. Lavette. Candidates—E. W. Johnson, Isaac Buggs.

To Examine Candidates in Fourth Year's Studies—B. W. Roberts, M. M. Moore, Fuller White. Candidates—S. L. C. Dawson, V. B. Brooks.

MODE OF TRIAL.

1st, The complainant presents his charge or complaint in person or by his counsel, and if there is no demurrer offered to it by the defendant or counsel,

2nd, Then the defendant is asked to plead to the complaint or charge. Should he plead guilty, there will be no need of any evidence being offered; but should he plead not guilty, then the complainant shall present his evidence or witness or witnesses, who shall be cross-examined by the defendant.

3rd, After which the defendant shall produce his witnesses, who shall be cross-examined by the counsel for the complainant; and when the evidence is closed, the counsel for the complainant opens the argument. The counsel for the defendant shall reply. Then the counsel for the complainant shall close the argument. The defendant shall retire, and then the Conference shall vote whether the allegation is sustained.

ANNUAL FEES OF THE CONFERENCE MISSIONARY SOCIETY, 1883.

A. W. Wayman	$1 00	S. L. Mims	$1 00
H. Call	1 00	F. White	50
A. Attaway	1 00	A. B. Dudley	1 00
A. J. Kershaw	1 00	M. A. Trapp	1 00
G. W. Witherspoon	1 00	George Anderson	1 00
W. A. Bird	1 00	J. H. Spears	1 00
L. Hargret	1 00	J. Speight	50
Isaac Buggs	25	John Taylor	50
Thomas Moorer	50	F. Lavette	55
J. H. Gilbert	1 00	A. Hammonds	50
E. Smith	1 00	M. M. Moore	50
A. Godwin	50	C. Brown	50
D. Quarterman	1 00	S. L. C. Dawson	1 00
Benj. Williams	50	W. C. Hamilton	50

J. P. Campbell	50	Edmund Robertson	1 00
F. J. Thompson	1 00	W. A. Burch	1 00
R. Raymon	15	E. W. Johnson	1 00
Wm. Washington	50	V. B. Brooks	25
Surry Lewis	25	Noah Randolph	50
L. W. Allen	1 00	C. L. Lane	1 00
Prince Williams	1 00	S. W. Frazier	1 00
John Dash	35	A. B. Collins	1 00
Fagan Peters	1 00	Charles Spires	25
P. Johnson	50	K. P. Neal	50

REPORTS.

REPORT ON TEMPERANCE.

*To the Bishop and Conference:—Dear Brethren:—*Your Committee to consider the subject of Temperance beg leave to submit the following. St. Paul said there was no law against temperance; therefore, a good temperance person is a fit temple for the indwelling of the Spirit of God, but an intemperate person has no room in his soul for the Spirit of the living God. Can sweet and bitter waters come from the same fountain? No. Can one servant serve two masters at once? No. Neither can the Spirit of God and the spirit of whiskey dwell in the same temple. We are sorry to say that the bottle has destroyed more souls than even the cannon or the sword, yet ministers of Christ are seen drinking that awful cup of hell. How can they say to the people, Thou shalt not steal? Do not you steal? Thou shalt not drink. Don't you drink? Leave it; oh, leave off now and forever.

Not only whiskies and other drinks are intemperance, but tobacco, cigars, pipes and snuff. Whosoever smokes or chews tobacco inflames the mind—degrades the pocket. Poverty and want are all in and around the house. Snuff is another destroyer of the lungs—debases the mind and shortens the life. Oh, how useless it is! Our ladies spend enough money for snuff, to educate all their children. We learn of a man whose tobacco bill annually is $50; his wife's snuff bill $20, which has been going on for sixteen years. A good many of our children are walking the streets, half naked—no hat nor shoes upon their heads or feet; yet their mothers and fathers can always find money to buy tobacco, cigars, pipe, snuff, or a bottle of whiskey.

Oh, ye ministers, we appeal to you first. Stop this unfit and useless habit of using tobacco; for a temperance person, one numbered with the blessed company—St. Paul—says, in the 1st chapter and 22nd verse of Galatians, to wit : " But the fruit of the Spirit is love, joy, peace, long suffering, gentleness, goodness, faith, meekness, temperance ; against such there is no law."

All of which is most respectfully submitted.

A. B. DUDLEY, Chairman,
C. F. BROWN.
GEORGE ANDERSON.
L. HARGRET.

REPORT ON EDUCATION.

*To the Bishop and Conference :—Dear Father and Brethren :—*It is said that Cato, a Roman Senator, feeling that the destruction of Carthage was necessary to the success of Rome, would, at every opportunity, cry aloud in **open** Senate, *"Carthago delenda est"* (Carthage must be destroyed). **It is** said that Wendell Phillips, when asked how the handfull **of** Abolitionists could possibly succeed against the millions who favored and sustained slavery, replied : "By agitation! agitation! agitation!" We do not fear the so-called majority. We are for the right ; therefore, God is with us ; and God and one in the right make a majority. Your Committee feel that, like Cato, our cry should unceasingly be, "Ignorance must be destroyed ;" and we feel that we can accomplish its destruction only by agitation. Your Committee also feel that the cause of Christian education is the cause of God. Therefore, we can press forward in its advocacy ; for if God be for us, he is more than all that may be against us. Methodism is a natural friend to education. The Wesleys and Whitfield, and a few others, while students in college, came to feel the necessity of having power, as well as the form of godliness, and began their meetings for praise and prayer, and the earnest study of God's Word, while dwelling within the enclosures of the college walls. It was their fellow-students who sneeringly called John and Charles, and their followers, Methodists. Your Committee would have this fact to be constantly borne in mind : The sainted founders of Methodism taught, both by precept and example, that the head, the understanding, as well as the heart, the soul, must enter into the service of God. One of the first things which Wesley did was to establish a school for the education of men for the ministry ; and that other great apostle of Methodism, our own beloved Bishop Allen, though himself limited as to his education, yet we understand that he conducted, as best he could, a night school in Philadelphia. Your Committee do not think it necessary to dwell on the importance of education, on its nature, or on its advantages. All of us acknowledge the comprehensiveness of the term education. Coming, as it does, from the Latin preposition "E," and the Latin verb *duco*, it signifies the development of the whole man—the body, the mind, and the heart. A simple knowledge of Greek and Latin, of science or philosophy, of mathematics or theology, of law, or of medicine, does not make a man educated ; but because if he has developed a comparatively healthy body, if by study his mind is trained, and if above all his heart is full of the love of God, then is he an example of the blessing of education, and his devotion to the cause of God, Christ, humanity, is the ruling principle of his everyday life.

Brethren, your Committee would have you hear the sound of the trumpet. It reverberates through the land, "Educate!" "Educate!" Hark! do the Florida Conference not hear our sentries—Payne, Wayman, Lee—cry, "To the work!" "To the work!" It is ringing through the connection from the lakes to the gulf, and from the silvery tide of the Atlantic to the golden shore of California. The various denominations are moving in battle array against the host of ignorance. The school house is the gun ; the teacher, the educated preacher, is the soldier ; and the Book and Cato, are powder and shot. Witness the educational institutions of the Methodist Episcopal Church, of the Baptists, of the Presbyterians, of the Congregationalists, of even the Roman Catholics. Their school houses are found in our cities, our towns, our villages, even out in our woods. From these places of learning thousands of preachers, teachers and children are going, year after year, to influence thought, and, therefore, to control the movements of men. Your committee are firmly of the opinion that just as the inflated balloon rises towards the skies, the tendency of the rising and coming generations, filled with knowledge, will be toward the churches promoting education ; and, brethren, we cannot be satisfied with only such acquisitions as come to us out of academies, colleges and seminaries sustained by other denominations. This kind of supply is not even now equal to the demand. We must raise within the bosom of our own church men and women who are to perpetuate our work, or we must fall victims to the law of the survival of the fittest, and pass away under the operation of the law of absorption, which, though slow, is sure—yes, terribly sure. No wonder that the Congregationalists say, "We are not in a hurry to organize churches. Numbers are not always strength. We shall educate now, and we know what the future will bring forth for Congregationalism in the South." There are some brethren in the Methodist Episcopal Church who are of the opinion that this glorious Communion of ours, founded by the sainted Allen, and now led by that great educator, Payne, will pass back into the mother church by the law of absorption ; that the M. E. Church, as the fat kine, will devour the A. M. E. Church, the lean kine ; and so they will, brethren, unless we cry with all our mind, soul and strength, "*Ignorantia delenda est*" (Ignorance must be destroyed).

Your Committee, in conclusion, beg leave to offer the following resolutions :

Resolved, That we reassert our heartfelt interest in the cause of education.

Resolved, That we shall, as far as practicable, organize educational and literary societies in colleges, whether they be circuits or stations ; hold monthly meetings for our mental improvement, and for raising, without making it burdensome, money for our educational wants.

2

Resolved, **That** we shall do all we can towards aiding and sustaining Wilberforce University, and our other connectional educational interests; and, at the same time, work earnestly to establish a College, or Conference High School, in this State.

Resolved, That hereafter candidates for admission into the Itinerancy, and for Holy Orders, shall be compelled to exhibit proficiency in **the** studies laid down in the Book of Discipline ; and any committee departing from this standard, and recommending incompetent candidates, shall be deemed guilty of wilful neglect of duty, and shall be liable to a vote of censure, and a reprimand in open Conference by the Bishop presiding.

All of which we respectfully submit.
M. M. Moore, Chairman.

REPORT **ON** SUNDAY SCHOOLS.

Monticello, Fla., December 2, **1882.**

To the Bishop and Conference :—We, your Committee, to whom was referred the subject of Sabbath Schools, having had the same under consideration, ask leave to submit the following report :

Sunday Schools are, beyond doubt, the nurseries of the Church. Without them, we have no assurance of permanent stability in our work: but with them, we can realize a confident hope of success in establishing happy homes and an improved state of society. Your Committee will further state that each pastor, who feels the care of the coming Church, should instruct our youth in the doctrine of Methodism ; and further recommend that our own system of Lessons, as taught in "Turner's Catechism" and "Child's Recorder," published by our Publishing Department, be the standard in all our schools.

Resolved, That Sabbath Schools must be organized in all parts of our work where **as** many as ten children can be gathered for that purpose.

Resolved, That all our ministers go forth from this Annual Conference resolved to do more in organizing and building up Sabbath Schools in our churches.

Resolved, further, That no minister or ministers of our Conference will be considered in good standing who wilfully neglects to feed the younger portion of his congregation—the lambs whom Jesus commands them to feed and care for.

All of which is respectfully submitted.
B. C. Gibbs,
F. J. Thompson,
Isaac Buggs.

REPORT ON PUBLICATION DEPARTMENT.

To the Bishop and Conference:—We, your Committee on Publication Department, beg leave to report the following :

We pen our recognition of the power of the press as a factor in individual and national elevation, and we express what experience has long since taught, that a people to be intelligent must of necessity be a reading people. In no department does genius more fully display itself at the close of the nineteenth century, than in the great field of literature. Its tongue is legion, and its voice like the sound of many waters, inviting people to closer thought, and keener analysis, and more profound reflection, touching questions of public policy both in Church and State, as well as the social community. It is anticipated that the pen is mightier than the sword : the well conducted newspaper is more powerful than an army with banners Therefore, we recommend that our preachers pursue a general course of reading, that they may become broadened in thought and liberal in sentiment. Our own publication, the *Christian Recorder*, should be in the homes of every family of our connection; also, the *Child's Recorder* should be in the hands of all our children. Further we recommend that our ministers do all within their power to circulate our Hymn Books and Discipline among our people, in order that they may know what we are doing to produce a literature for our Church and race. We are also sorry to say that there are a great many of our ordained ministers who fail to patronize our own Publication Department, and are actually engaged in opposition against it, saying it is too high-priced.

Resolved, That we, the members of the Florida Annual Conference, do all within our power to aid said Publication Department.

Resolved, further, That we have the utmost confidence in the present Manager, Rev. T. Gould, for the able manner in which he has been and is conducting our Publication Department.

Respectfully,　　　　　　　　　　E. R. ROBINSON, Chairman,
　　　　　　　　　　　　　　　　THOS. MOORER,
　　　　　　　　　　　　　　　　A. ATTAWAY.

The following is the Manager's annual report for the year 1882 :

MANAGER'S ANNUAL REPORT FOR 1882.

To the Presiding Bishop and Members of the West Florida Annual Conference:—This comes greeting. Through the kind providence of Almighty God, I have been spared to complete my second annual report of the Publishing Department, which I have the honor to represent. Said report will be found in full in the Financial Secretary's "Budget" for 1882, which shows the following results :

```
Balance from last year....................................$   311 08
Receipts during year......................................  15,662 26

    Total...................................................$15,973 34
Expenses during year......................................  15,713 10

    Balance...............................................$   260 24
```

Assets—Including amount due on *Recorder, Child's Recorder,*
   and *S. S. Lessons,* printing furniture and plates..........$25,062 59
Liabilities—Including debts contracted before and during
   present administration..................................... 8,320 07

Excess of assets over liabilities.............................$16,742 52

The press of business at the Office makes it almost imperative for
me to be present the most of my time in order that promptness to
business may be secured. I therefore will be unable to attend your
present session. Hoping you may have a profitable session, I remain
your humble servant,   THEO. GOULD,
                                Manager.

The Finance Committee made the following report :

REPORT OF FINANCE COMMITTEE.

```
Contingent money from churches............................$15 35
Public collection...........................................  64 56

    Total amount collected.................................$79 91
    Total disbursements, to wit :
Stationery................................................$  4 00
Bishop's traveling expenses...............................  40 00
Sexton...................................................   2 75
Freight on "Budget".......................................   3 60
Committee on Railroad.....................................   3 00
Expenses of the Parsonage................................   3 05
Church expenses, lights, &c...............................     50
Pastoral Credentials......................................   5 00
Two Elders' Credentials...................................   1 00
Three Deacons' Credentials................................     60
                                                          -------
                                                          $63 50
```

Balance on hand.....   16 41

```
Missionary money collected from churches..................$10 75
From members of Conference Missionary Society.............  33 15

    Total Missionary money collected......................$43 90
Forty per cent. sent to J. M. Townsend....................$18 16
Sixty per cent. retained in Conference....................  25 74
                                                          -------
                                                          $43 90

Received from Dollar Money.................................$58 60
The sixty per cent. Missionary money added................  25 74

    Total balance on hand.................................$84 34
```
    All of which is respectfully submitted.

                              J. H. SPEARS, Chairman.

Committee on Contingent reported the following:

A. B. Dudley,...	$1 00	A. J. Kershaw..	$ 50	A. R. Handsberry..$	25
E. W. Johnson,...	25	B. C. Gibbs,.....	25	F. Lavette,........	1 00
W. C. Hamilton,..	25	M. A. Trapp,....	1 00	J. H. Spears,......	50
W. A. Byrd,......	1 00	J. H. Gilbert....	30	Isaac Bugg, ...	50
L. W. Allen......	25	Thos. Moorer,...	25	J. P. Campbell,....	25
Geo. Washington..	25	G. W. T. Wynn..	25	Wm. Washington,..	50
P. Croom,........	25	A. Hammonds,..	30	E. R. Roberson,....	30
S. W. Frazier,........		C. Brown,.......	50	Surry Lewis,.......	15
D. Quarterman,..	1 00	W. A. Burch,....	30	C. B. Green,.......	25
C. L. Lane,.......	30	M. M. Moore,....	25	L. Hargret,........	25
J. Churchill,........		E. Smith,........	25	F. White,..........	50
J. Speight,........	1 00	A. D. Spears,....	25	B. W. Roberts,........	
J. Hardy,............		Geo. Anderson,..	25	Navy Yard,...	
F. J. Thompson, ...		J. Taylor,........	50	Smith Dawson,.	15
V. B. Brooks,........		T. W. Dawkins,.	10	A. Attaway,...........	

$15 35
64 56

Total amount..$79 91

BOOK STEWARD'S REPORT.

*To the Bishop and Conference:—Dear Brethren:—*Your Book Steward begs leave to report, That I have received the following named books from Rev. T. Gould and sold the same, to wit:

40 Hymn Books; 45 Disciplines; 30 Wayman on Discipline; 46 Wayman's Recollections; 2 Hints to a Self-Educated Minister; 3 Not a Man, yet a Man; 2 Theological Compends; 36 Class Books; 3 Bishop Allen's Life; 6 Prize Essays; 260 Turner's Catechisms; 100 Local Preachers' Licenses; 100 Little Learner's Papers; 100 Scholar's Quarterly, and 2 Superintendent's Quarterly—a total of 100 stories of the Gospel—$74.00.

Also have the following cash subscribers to the *Christian Recorder:*
Rev. A. B. Dudley, A. R. Hansberry, R. Raymon, J. H. Spears, A. Attaway, S. L. Mims, G. W. T. Wynns, D. Quarterman, Edmund Smith, John Churchwell, W. A. Burch, L. Hargret, James Clark, Joseph Hardy, F. J. Thompson, C. L. Lane, Adam Thompson, V. B. Brooks, Joseph Cobbs, F. White, and A. Godwin.

I have visited as far as possible, lecturing and selling books for our Departments. Many of the pastors assisted greatly in selling books, while others have acted very coldly. The "Recollections" sells well, and should be read in every Methodist family. The "Turner Catechism" has a ready sale in all of our Sunday Schools. The *Christian*

Recorder is the organ of our Church, and should be used by every preacher, superintendent, and friends of the A. M. E. Church.

Resolved, That every member of this Conference take that paper, so as to keep himself informed of the general news of the Church.

With much success to the A. M. E. Church Department, I have the honor to be yours, A. B. DUDLEY,
Conference Book Steward.

REPORT ON BILLS.

*To the Bishop and Conference:—Dear Brethren:—*Yours appointed to collect bills against some of the members of this Conference, beg leave to report, That I have examined them, and have found the following indebted to the Publishing Department, to wit:

Rev. J. H. Gilbert... $3 60
Rev. G. W. T. Wynns... 99
Rev. J. H. Spears... 40 25

Makes a total of... $44 **84**

Rev. J. H. Gilbert and G. W. T. Wynns have settled their bills.

Also the following bills against brethren of the East Conference:

Rev. J. W. Bowen... $ 7 **50**
Rev. P. L. Cuyler.. 8 **25**
Rev. R. W. Butler... 5 **04**
Rev. W. C. Cole... 5 **40**

A total of.. $26 19

Which I do respectfully return them to Elder C. H. Pierce to collect when his Conference meets. Respectfully,
A. B. **DUDLEY.**

REPORT ON THIRD YEAR'S STUDIES.

*To the Bishop and Conference:—*We, your Committee appointed to examine the third year class, beg leave to make the following report, to wit: We have had before us Brothers E. W. Johnson and Isaac Buggs, and have carefully examined them on reading, writing, orthography, geography, and on the doctrines of the Bible; also, arithmetic; and find that they have a splendid knowledge of the above mentioned studies. Therefore, we recommend that they be elected to Elders orders.

Respectfully, THOMAS MOORER, Chairman,
F. LAVETTE,
W. A. BYRD.

REPORT ON CHARGES AND COMPLAINTS.

*To the Bishop and Conference:—*We, your Committee appointed on Charges and Complaints, beg leave to make the following report, to wit: We had before us Brother M. A. Trapp, to whom a charge was referred, against him; and after careful examination of the same, discovered that it was best to refer it back to the Conference.

Respectfully, THOMAS MOORER, Chairman,
J. H. GILBERT,
D. QUARTERMAN.

TOTAL DISBURSEMENT OF THE BOARD OF DIRECTORS **OF THE** CONFERENCE MISSIONARY SOCIETY.

Paid W. L. G. Jones	$4 00	Am't brought forward	$47 00
" H. Call	2 00	Paid George Washington	2 00
" R. Meacham	4 00	" S. L. C. Dawson	3 00
" F. White	2 00	" William Washington	2 00
" A. J. Kershaw	1 00	" C. B. Green	3 00
" A. B. Dudley	2 00	" B. C. Gibbs	2 00
" George Anderson	2 00	" W. C. Hamilton	2 00
" A. L. Hargrett	3 00	" J. P. Campbell	1 00
" J. Taylor	2 00	" Cæsar Clory	1 00
" Thomas Moorer	2 00	" E. Roberson	1 00
" J. H. Gilbert	1 00	" F. J. Thompson	3 00
" P. Crooms	4 00	" W. A. Burch	2 00
" A. Hammonds	2 00	" Robert Rayman	50
" E. Smith	2 00	" V. B. Brooks	1 00
" H. B. DeVaughn	5 00	" S. W. Frazier	1 00
" Alex. Godwin	5 00	" L. W. Allen	1 00
" C. Brown	1 00	" G. W. T. Wynns	1 00
" D. Quarterman	1 00	" C. L. Lane	1 00
" A. R. Hansberry	2 00		
	$47 00	Total	$74 50

THOMAS MOORER, Secretary.

REPORT ON ·DOLLAR MONEY.

The Committee on Dollar Money made the following report of collections, to wit:

Monticello Station	$40 00	Chattahoochee Mission	6 00
Thompson Valley Circuit	27 00	Waukulla Mission	3 50
Ancilla "	15 60	Lake Jackson Circuit	17 00
Wankeenah "	25 00	Walker Mission	9 56
Union Hill "	26 50	Mount Pleasant Station	5 00
Turkey Scratch "	20 00	Marianna Station	16 00
Monticello Mission	16 50	Antioch Station	8 10
Concord, Leon Circuit	28 00	Campbellton Station	12 00
Centenary "	28 00	Springfield Station	18 00
Centreville "	30 00	Greenwood Circuit	18 00
Station One "	20 00	Mount Olive, Jackson Co	5 00
Gum Swamp "	34 00	Jerusalem Mission	2 00
Mount Olive "	30 00	Liberty County Mission	6 00
Tallahassee Station	33 00	Bethlehem Station	18 50
St. Johns Circuit	20 00	Apalachicola Station	30 00
Tallahassee Mission	1 00	Aspalaga Mission	5 38
Quincy Station	8 00	Pensacola Mission	3 00
Concord, Gadsden County	10 00	Walton County Mission	10 00
Rock Comfort Mission	10 00	Milton Station	2 50
Midway Circuit	4 00	Washington County Mission	29 00
Imonia Slough Mission	5 00		

Total amount Dollar Money collected $655 54

Amount brought to Conference $655 54
Thirty per cent. retained in Conference 196 66

Amount forwarded Financial Secretary $458 88

A. J. KERSHAW, Secretary.
G. W. WITHERSPOON, Chairman.

A. W. WAYMAN, Presiding Bishop.

REPORT ON SUPERANNUATED PREACHERS, WIDOWS AND ORPHANS' CLAIMS.

The Committee on Superannuated Preachers, Widows and Orphans' Claims made the following report, to wit : We find nine widows, three superannuated preachers, and one orphan, and recommend that they be paid the following amount, which was done :

Sent Jane Argret per J. H. Spears	$10	00
" Minerva Hall per T. Moorer	15	00
" Nancy Mathews per J. H. Gilbert	12	00
" Annie McGriff per J. H. Gilbert	10	00
" Ann Livingston per F. White	10	00
" Maria Clemings per F. White	12	00
" Mary Livingston per F. White	15	00
" Rocksey Godwin per L. Hargrett	10	00
" Amanda Wood per J. Taylor	5	00
" J. Churchill per H. Call	10	00
" Orphan child per A. W. Wayman	10	00
Paid to Benjamin Williams	12	00
" " Allen Jones, Sr	10	00
Total amount	$141	00

F. Lavette, Chairman.

LIST OF MEMBERS

Who paid the one dollar of the Dollar **Money**, 1882, of Waukeenah **A. M. E. Church Circuit :**

Henry Deggs	$1 00	James Bassa	$1 00
Sarah Reden	1 00	James Denmark	1 00
Theo. Cole	1 00	Pattie Bassa	1 00
Council Kilpatrick	1 00	Anna Hall	1 00
Betsy Kilpatrick	1 00	Lettie Roberts	1 00
Silvey Cole	1 00	Ussa Williams	1 00
Matilda Smith	1 00	Eliza McCall	1 00
Isaiah Brown	1 00	Rebecca Roberts	1 00
William Walden	1 00	Lydia Edwards	1 00
Frank Allen	1 00	John Howel	1 00
Peggy Allen	1 00	Peggy Howel	1 00
D. W. Robinson	1 00	Nellie Deggs	1 00
Maria Brown	1 00	Elizzie Roberson	1 00

A. B. Dudley, Pastor.

RECAPITULATION.

Itinerant Preachers	67
Local Preachers	142
Exhorters	50
Full Members	4,555
Probationers	808
Sabbath School Scholars	4,426
Sabbath Schools	70
Churches	56
Parsonages	20
Value Church Property	$23,403 00
Books in S. S. Library	2,758
Dollar Money	$655 54
Contingent Money	79 91
Missionary Money	42 90
Educational Money	6 85
Mite Missionary Money	1 90
Paid to Preachers, Widows and Orphans	204 00
Conference Expenses	63 50
Pastors' Support	5,966 79
Presiding Elders' Support	1,108 28
Sabbath School Money	272 10

GENERAL OFFICERS OF A. M. E. CHURCH.

EPISCOPAL DISTRICTS.

1st District—J. M. Brown, D. D., D. C. L.
2nd District—D. A. Payne, D. D., LL. D.
3rd District—J. A. Shorter.
4th District—T. M. D. Ward, D. D.
5th District—J. P. Campbell, D. D., LL. D.
6th District—W. F. Dickerson, D. D.
7th District—A. W. Wayman, D. D.
8th District—H. M. Turner, D. D., LL. D.
9th District—R. H. Cain, D. D.

General Business Manager—Theo. Gould.
Editor Christian Recorder—B. T. Tanner, D. D.
Secretary Missionary Society—J. M. Townsend.
Secretary Education—B. F. Watson.
President Wilberforce University—B. F. Lee, D. D.
Secretary Sunday School Union—C. S. Smith.

COLLEGES.

WILBERFORCE UNIVERSITY.

FACULTY.

Rev. B. F. Lee, D. D., President.
J. P. Shorter, A. M., Professor of Mathematics.
W. S. Scarborough, Professor Latin and Greek.
R. F. Howard, A. B., B. L., Professor Law.
John Little, Professor Law.
Mrs. S. C. Bierce, Instructor in Natural Sciences.
Miss G. E. Clark, Teacher of Instrumental Music.
Anna H. Jones, Teacher of Elocution.
Rev. J. G. Mitchell, D. D., General Agent.

ALLEN UNIVERSITY.

J. C. Waters, D. D., President.
Professor—J. W. Morris.
Mrs. E. A. Pindle.
Miss Bertha Wolfe.

PAUL QUINN COLLEGE.

Bishop R. H. Cain, D. D., President.
W. R. Carson, Secretary.
H. Wilhite, Treasurer.

Meeting of Trustees of Brown University.

MONTICELLO, FLA., December 6, 1882.

At half-past 3 o'clock P. M., the Trustees of the above named College met. Rev. A. B. Dudley called the meeting to order.

On motion of D. Quarterman, W. L. JONES was elected Chairman, and A. B. DUDLEY, Secretary.

Elder C. H. Pearce, of the East Florida Conference, was asked to state the condition of the lands belonging to Brown University, which he did, stating that said property was in danger of falling into other hands unless the Conference would go to work and free it from a small debt that was now upon it.

On motion of S. L. Mims, each pastor was requested to collect one dollar immediately and forward the same to A. Attaway, Monticello, Fla., to pay said debt.

On motion of S. L. Mims, W. L. G. Jones and A. B. Dudley were appointed a committee of two to confer with the members of the East Florida Conference in relation to the condition of the said Brown University.

On motion, the meeting adjourned.

The foregoing is a true copy of the Florida Annual Conference of the A. M. E. Church for the year 1882.

A. **W.** WAYMAN, *Presiding Bishop.*

A. J. KERSHAW, *Secretary.*

ROLL OF MEMBERS.

Bishop, A. W. WAYMAN, D. D.

PRESIDING ELDERS.

A. Attaway, Fuller White, T. Moorer,
W. L. Jones.

TRAVELING ELDERS.

H. Call,	R. Meacham,	W. G. Stewart,
A. J. Kershaw,	A. B. Dudley,	M. A. Trapp.
G. W. Witherspoon,	George Anderson,	W. A. Byrd.
J. H. Spears,	L. Hargret,	J. Speight,
I. Buggs,	J. Taylor,	F. Lavette.
Peter Crooms,	A. Hammonds,	E. Smith,
H. B. DeVaughn,	Alex. Godwin,	C. Brown,
D. Quarterman.	A. R. Hansberry,	S. L. C. Dawson,
	E. W. Johnson.	

TRAVELING DEACONS.

George Washington,	C. B. Green,	B. C. Gibbs.
W. C. Hamilton,	C. L. Clory,	J. P. Campbell,
Edmund Robertson,	F. J. Thompson,	C. L. Lane,
W. A. Burch.	T. W. Dawkins,	R. Raymon.
G. W. Wynn.	S. W. Frazer.	

LICENTIATES.

W. Washington,	J. E. Roberts,	Surry Lewis,
John Holland.	Noah Randolph,	L. W. Allen,
John Dash,	H. Humphreys,	Henry Starks,
A. D. Collins,	K. P. Neal,	F. Peters,
C. Spires,	James Clark.	

LOCAL ELDERS.

Henry Hall, B. Nathan, **Noah Graham.**

LOCAL DEACONS.

F. Barton. S. Marshall, M. Roberts.
George Hawkins.

SUPERANNUATED PREACHERS.

Allen Jones, Benjamin Williams, John Churchill.

PUBLISHING COMMITTEE.

Rev. A. B. DUDLEY, - - - Chairman and Treasurer.
Rev. A. J. KERSHAW, - - - - - - - Secretary.
Rev. T. MOORER, - - - - - - - - Recorder.
D. QUARTERMAN, - - - - - - - Statistician.

Minutes must sell for **10 cents per copy**.